Philippe Fix

Seraphin

translated from the French by
Donald Nicholson-Smith

SERAPHIN

HERCULES

PLUME

elsewhere
editions

When Seraphin reached the age when he had to decide what he was going to be, he faced a problem as serious as it was complicated: what career should he choose?

Chief Executive Officer? Not likely with that haircut!

Big-game hunter? Hardly. Seraphin couldn't hurt a fly.

Deep-sea diver perhaps? No: Seraphin always got seasick on boats.

Police officer? Seraphin hated guns.

Firefighter? Seraphin was a really deep sleeper. No siren would ever wake him up.

Santa Claus? The slightest chill gave Seraphin a terrible cold.

What then? In the end, Seraphin applied for a job as a ticket puncher in the Paris Metro.

"Have you ever punched tickets anywhere else?" he was asked.

"No," said Seraphin.

"Well, come again tomorrow. We'll try you out and see how you do."

Back at home, Seraphin spent the evening practicing. He punched holes in everything he could lay his hands on, from the rent receipt to his best Sunday necktie.

By the next Monday, he was hired.

At first, Seraphin loved his job. It was fun watching the trains coming through one after the other. Every three minutes at rush hour; every eight minutes for normal service; and every quarter of an hour during slow periods.

But one day, he didn't know why, Seraphin found the people sad, the subway cars sad, the station sad. What could he do? Be sad too? Impossible. Seraphin was a born optimist.

So what did he do? He brought flowers to work and decorated his ticket puncher's booth with them. They were pretty, and they smelled wonderful. Suddenly the sunshine seemed to have come down into the Metro station.

But nobody appeared to notice the transformation. True, the passengers always kept their eyes to the ground!

Did I say nobody? Not quite: the station master did not miss a thing.

"One more bright idea like this, Mister Seraphin," he said, "and I'll report you to the intern of the assistant to the adjunct commissary of my superior officer!"

From then on, Seraphin spent the better part of his time merely dreaming of flowers, birds, and sunshine. The little holes that up until now he had tried to punch in the exact middle of each ticket now tended to stray towards the side. Sometimes he even punched only half-holes on the very edge. All the same... All the same, when quitting time came, Seraphin broke into a smile just as soon as he got out of his uniform. After a long day in his underground prison, he could not wait to get back to his attic in the old part of Paris.

Seraphin lived in a little room on the top floor of a big apartment building. Seven flights was a considerable number of stairs! Seraphin was particularly fond of the hundred and twenty-sixth one. Unlike all the others it creaked, and, what was more, this meant that there were only two more flights to go. As for the very last stair, it was Seraphin's very favorite.

Way up at the top of the building, Plume would be listening out for the sound of Seraphin's footsteps. Seraphin was Plume's friend, and Plume could not wait to see him.

"Is that you, Plume? Hi!"

"Hi. I've been expecting you," Plume would answer, half cocooned in an amazing sweater in whose depths his hamster Hercules would often take up residence.

Seraphin loved to tinker. A few scraps of wood or paper, and some glue, and from his hands would emerge a toy or an ingenious gadget.

Hercules had a little treadmill on which he would trot as all hamsters do. Seraphin transformed it into a real whirligig. As soon as the wheel turned all the moving parts were set in motion. Hercules was thrilled!

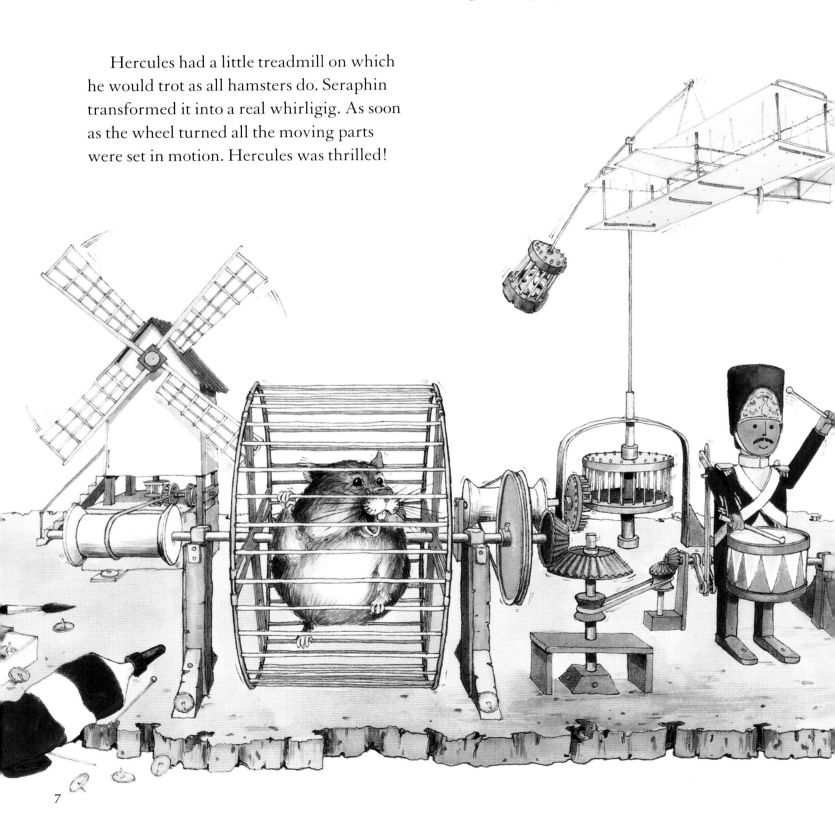

On fine days Seraphin and Plume loved to stroll through the picturesque aisles of the flea market, where chance brings the most varied objects together. A Normandy armoire may be found next to a corkscrew, or a bust of Socrates alongside military medals.

And so it was that one day Seraphin came upon the bed he had been dreaming of from his earliest childhood: a four-poster with wooden barley-sugar columns and ornamental golden angels to watch over the sleeper.

Alas, just imagine the disappointment of our friend when, after concluding his purchase with the seller, he found out that the bed would not fit into his mansard-roofed bedroom. He tried to set it up lengthwise, sideways, even crossways, but nothing worked. Seraphin had no choice but to dismantle the bed and store it on the seventh-floor landing, to the fury of his neighbor, a butcher by trade, who threatened to slice it up like salami!

When Monday came, with his cap on his head and his ticket punch in hand, Seraphin went back to work.

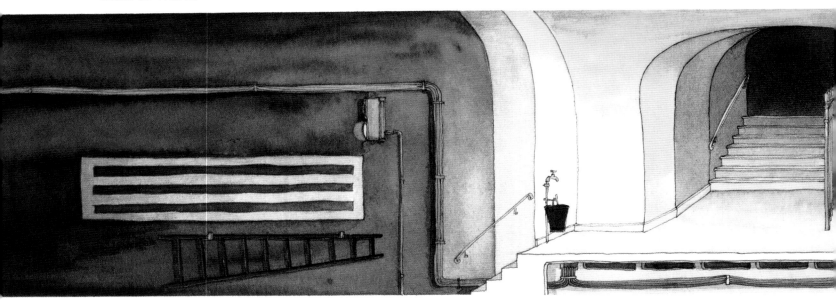

"Oh!" he thought once rush hour was over, "what would I not give to be done with this groundhog's life! To live at last in daylight, to flit through the open air like a butter —"

All of a sudden Seraphin had to rub his eyes. Was it possible? Down here in the tunnel a butterfly was fluttering along.

"Poor thing! What will become of it in these endless mole tunnels? He'll never find his way back to the daylight and the sun's tender touch...I must set it free."

And without hesitation Seraphin raced off, cap at the ready to catch the lost butterfly. Why did a group of passengers have to pick that very moment to show up at his abandoned booth?

And why ever did the station master decide at that very same moment to inspect the platform?

Five minutes later, the butterfly and Seraphin were both enjoying newfound freedom in the avenues of the city. Both had been escorted out of the Metro in short order, the former by the latter and the latter by the station master.

How long did Seraphin wander through sun-filled streets, flower-adorned squares and parks resonant with birdsong? No one can say. Not even Seraphin.

In any case, when he got home, he was surprised to find a letter pushed under his door. A lawyer was asking Seraphin to pay him a visit as soon as possible.

"Now then," said the old man as soon as Seraphin was sitting in his dismal dusty office, "it is my pleasure to inform you that you have inherited a house. A structure that is very old now, in its own grounds and with several outbuildings, with respect to which I must tell you…"

Seraphin had stopped listening. He was thinking about how overjoyed Plume would be to hear this happy news.

"An old mansion!"

"A manor house!!"

"Maybe a chateau!!!"

But the very next morning, when the two visited the property, their dreams evaporated.

The house was a ruin.

But then Seraphin shrugged his shoulders and rolled up his sleeves.

"After all," he said, "a house in ruins is better than no house at all."

"Come quickly!" shouted Plume suddenly. "I've found something fantastic."

A car!

A car as dilapidated as the house, true, but a car just the same. Seraphin's view of the future was suddenly much rosier.

"Car, house, fresh air! Come on, Plume, there's not a moment to lose. Let's get to work!"

No sooner said than done. The old car was dismantled, de-dented, oiled, overhauled, rewelded, tightened up, repaired, improved, and reassembled.

When Plume started the motor, the machine ran as smoothly, in a word, as Hercules' treadmill.

With a vehicle like this, transporting the materials needed to restore the house would be child's play for our two friends.

I won't tell you how many trips they made. Suffice it to say that every single home-improvement store in the vicinity received a visit from them, that their car hauled exactly 52,291 pounds of all kinds of building materials, and that Seraphin's savings from his period of employment were completely used up.

As for how many hours our amateur architects worked on the scaffolding and how many hours wielding pick, trowel, or paintbrush, only the sun and moon could really say. The fact is, though, that one fine morning…

One fine morning, the outside work on the house was finished.

LOOK!

Seraphin was proud of his work, and he had every right to be. His house seemed to come out of a dream, and it was like no other house.

At long last he was able to set up his canopied bed.

Once its barley-sugar posts and its draperies were installed in all their glory, Seraphin put on his Sunday-best pajamas and slipped between the sheets.

The gilded wooden angels hardly needed to lull him that night: he fell asleep with a smile on his lips, utterly happy.

But what good was a house so beautiful to look at on the outside if it wasn't beautiful inside too? It was time to fix up the interior.

But Seraphin's savings were all gone, so money had to be made before any more expenses could be considered.

Seraphin built a pushcart with astonishing features. In summer he sold ice cream from it, and in winter sweet-smelling roasted chestnuts. The cart also had a grindstone for sharpening knives and scissors, and little drawers containing a host of labor-saving gadgets for use around the house. Seraphin would ring a little bell to announce his cart's arrival. Its tinkle was a friendly call and as soon as they heard it children would come running up.

"Here comes Old Seraphin!" they would cry. They might as easily have cried, "Here comes Santa Claus!"

After a few months of this, Seraphin and the ever-faithful Plume were able to start on the inside of the house.

"Let's see," said Seraphin one day. "Wherever did I put that paintbrush? I had it just a moment ago."

Plume, who was perched on a beam, could not refrain from answering:

"You're always losing your things, Seraphin. Why don't you do like me and knit yourself an all-purpose sweater? In the front it's a drawer, in the back it's a hamster's nest, and on the side…"

But, as practical as he was, Plume could not finish his sentence, for he suddenly lost his balance and toppled into thin air.

"And on the top," laughed Seraphin, "I suppose it's a parachute?"

By dint of patience and determination, Seraphin's house was at long last completely finished. Now that their work was done, how good it felt to our two friends to snooze by the great fireplace!

One evening, when Seraphin had nodded off in his rocking chair, something very strange happened. Plume was gazing at the flames licking at the logs on the fire when all of a sudden the sap as it burned produced a whistle that was low at first but increasingly high-pitched. At this magic signal, all the figures, sculpted or drawn, that their creators had fixed in solid form over so many years, began to move.

Plume rubbed his eyes when he saw a hot-air balloon leave its picture frame and fly around the house, but he rubbed them in vain. And the sharper the whistle grew, the greater the magical effect. The golden angels on Seraphin's four-poster took flight one by one, while the Three Musketeers left the pages of a large story book to rejoin Don Quixote and Sancho Panza. In the hearth the logs went on crackling and the sap went on singing.

"Hi there!" said Pinocchio as he jumped onto Plume's knee. "Have you seen my friend Harlequin by any chance?"

"Let's go, gentlemen," cried a fat June bug, tapping with his baton on the podium. "Back to the beginning of the symphony. A bar for nothing…"

For long afterwards Plume wondered if he had dreamt that enchanted evening or if the magic had really occurred. He never really knew the answer. Seraphin had been dozing in his chair the whole time, and otherwise everything seemed normal. Still, Seraphin's house was not exactly like other houses…

"Is that you, Plume? Hello. I was waiting for you."

Life at Seraphin's was truly wonderful. Every time Plume visited his friend he had the feeling he was entering a barn. An immense barn, full of mysterious corners, unsuspected hideaways, and endless surprises. You felt relaxed there, and you had an urge to sing.

But Plume sang off-key, and one day he drew his friend aside.

"Seraphin," he said, "a house without music is not a real house. We should…"

Seraphin hushed him with a gesture. He had noticed the lack too. And he had an idea.

"We are going to do something about that today, Plume. Start the car! The seller is open for business this morning."

"You mean the guy who sells radios?"

But Plume was way off the mark: Seraphin's idea was far better than that!

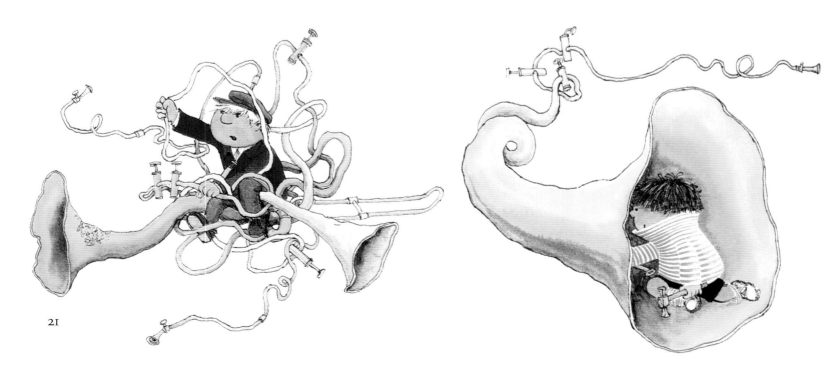

It took a whole week to gather everything needed from the scrap-metal seller's yard. After that Seraphin closed himself in the house and worked for two days and two nights without stopping. When at last Plume was allowed in to see Seraphin's work, he was thunderstruck.

"What would you like to hear?" asked the do-it-yourselfer seated at his control console. "A Bach suite? Buttons A, X, 23, Z, and there you are! A polka? Buttons B, M, 39, K, and off we go!"

The effect was astounding. A full-scale orchestra could not have played better — or louder. What was more, a special button had an effect very rarely produced even by an orchestra of virtuosi, namely silence!

This time Seraphin's happiness knew no bounds. Cozily installed in his house with his friend Plume, sometimes pottering, sometimes making music, and sometimes reading fabulous stories from an immense illustrated book, their life proceeded gently, calmly, and free of problems. This might easily have gone on for years and years if two men had not appeared one day with a letter covered with official stamps and seals.

At the sight of the fatter of the two, who immediately put him in mind of the station master from his days as a ticket puncher, Seraphin sensed right away that something was up. Something awful. He understood nothing of the visitors' explanations, but their strange, harsh words wounded him like so many poison arrows.

The men wagged their fingers at Seraphin in a threatening way before turning away. Their lethal words kept bouncing around in Seraphin's head: *eminent domain, recourse to justice, industrial zone, housing projects, reinforced concrete, court-ordered demolition, immediate departure …*

Before long, workmen arrived to chop down the tall trees that Seraphin and Plume so loved. Then came trucks, cranes and bulldozers.

Great gray masses of cement blocks then began springing up on every side, growing higher and higher with every day that passed. The noise became intolerable and dust and giant cranes blocked out the sun. Seraphin's house was caught in a terrifying pincer's grip of steel and reinforced concrete that was slowly strangling it to death.

Determined to defend their property at any cost, Plume and Seraphin holed up in the house, closing all the doors and windows.

The next time the two men came by, our two friends would not even let them in.

Seraphin could not help shuddering when he read the notice that they slipped beneath the door:

Final Warning: If you do not vacate these premises within 48 hours, we shall be obliged to call upon the legal authorities to enforce your eviction.

The law was the law. Would they have to obey?

In any case life had become unbearable. Whenever Seraphin and Plume slipped out to go shopping, the construction workers would taunt them. A machine operator even went so far as to threaten them with his enormous claw.

They had to do something.

Seraphin's first idea was to invent a gigantic robot.

"But you know," said Plume, "robots don't frighten anyone any more. What you should build is a dragon — a shimmering dragon with eyes that light up and with smoke and flames shooting out of its mouth. Just like the ones in stories."

"Okay!" said Seraphin. "Let's get to work!"

They chose a misty day to bring their dragon out. Its appearance on the construction site caused general panic. Everyone took to their heels, abandoning their machines, as if they had experienced a terrifying hallucination.

Sad to say, this success was short-lived.

The next day the two men came back to order Seraphin out. Their attempts to reason with him, telling him how comfortable modern buildings were, left him cold. Seraphin would never resign himself to seeing his home destroyed. He knew that nothing could replace the warmth of his old house.

So Seraphin barricaded himself inside with his friend Plume.

When the bailiffs knocked too loudly on the door, he sat down at the console of his orchestra-machine and played a deafening symphony.

Though the strains of the music delighted our two friends, the representatives of the law did not share their enthusiasm. They decreed the immediate eviction of the occupants, to be followed by the demolition of their home.

That was when Seraphin and Plume decided to make their escape. Since all the exits were under guard, they gathered all the lumber they could find and, without knowing quite what they were doing, began, plank by plank, to construct an immense tower above the roof of the house.

"Come down right away!" came shouts from below. "Or we'll get you down ourselves!"

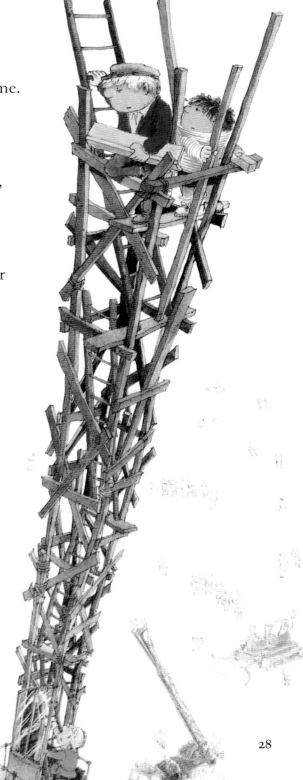

"It's useless to go on. You can't get away from us. Give up right now!"

Around the house a crowd had gathered and was getting ready to scoff at the fugitives when they came down with heads lowered, defeated.

"For the last time, I repeat, come down!"

But since Plume and Seraphin made no response and went on building, firemen were ordered to lay siege to the tower. They climbed to the top of their high ladder, then clambered onto the perilous structure. But the higher they got, the more vigorously our two friends persisted in their desperate ascent.

The firemen in front were already nearing the top; they were no more than a few strides away. A few seconds more, and they would reach the two friends and grab them.

It was then that Seraphin had a brilliant idea: by placing four stairs together, and then moving the bottom one over to the top, and repeating this time after time, Plume and Seraphin constructed a staircase that allowed them to leave the tower far behind.

Before the stupefied eyes of the suddenly silent crowd below, they were soon out of range of the highest rungs of the firemen's ladder. They soon reached the white clouds that mottled the sky. Eventually they were no more than a barely perceptible microscopic speck.

Seraphin and Plume were going far, far, far away.